When the Leaf Blew In

To the Umholtz Family —
Paige, Seth, Jolene, and Rich
— S.M.

To Grandpa, bunnies, and kittens.
— K.L.

ISBN 0-439-85931-X
Text copyright © 2006 by Steve Metzger
Illustrations copyright © 2006 by Kellie Lewis
All rights reserved. Published by Scholastic Inc.
SCHOLASTIC and associated logos are trademarks and/or registered
trademarks of Scholastic Inc.

12 11 10 9 8 7 6 5 4 3 2 1   6 7 8 9 10 11/0

Printed in the U.S.A.
First printing, September 2006

When the Leaf Blew In

by Steve Metzger
illustrated by Kellie Lewis

SCHOLASTIC INC.
New York   Toronto   London   Auckland   Sydney
Mexico City   New Delhi   Hong Kong   Buenos Aires

When the leaf blew in . . .
The cow sneezed, "Ah choo!"

When the cow sneezed, "Ah choo!" . . .
The spider landed on the owl!

When the spider landed on the owl . . .
The owl swooped out of the barn!

When the owl swooped out of the barn . . .
The pig dove into the mud!

When the pig dove into the mud . . .
The goat kicked over the bucket!

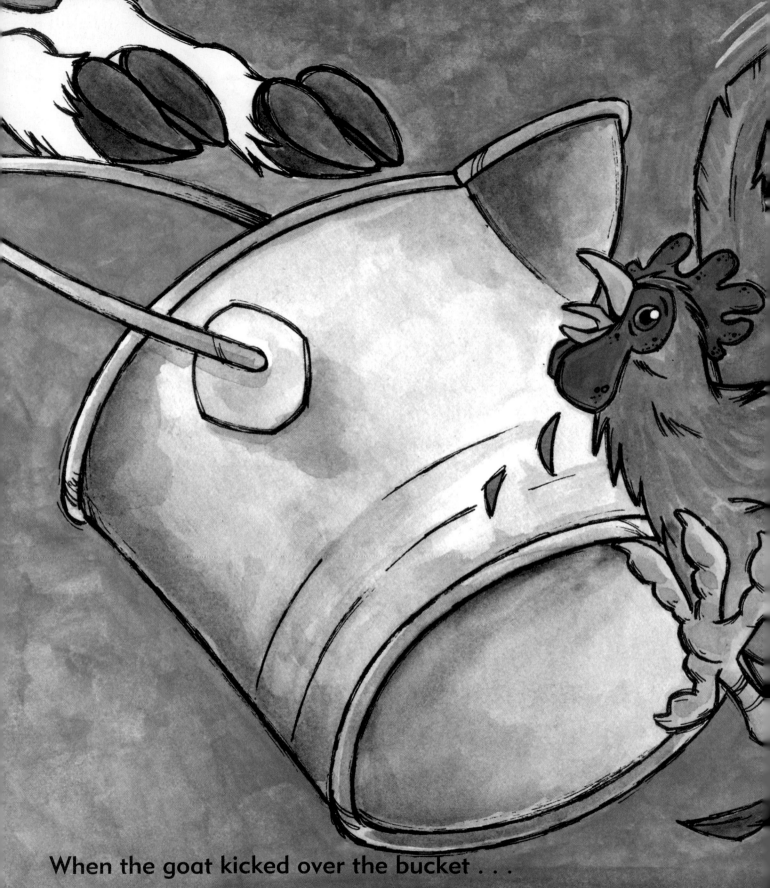

When the goat kicked over the bucket . . .
The chicken spun 'round and 'round!

When the chicken spun 'round and 'round . . .
The horse reared up and neighed!

When the horse reared up and neighed . . .
The sheep leaped over a barrel!

When the sheep leaped over a barrel . . .
The duck jumped into the pond!

When the duck jumped into the pond . . .
The frog hopped onto a lily pad!

When the frog hopped onto a lily pad . . .
The dragonfly buzzed across the sky!

When the dragonfly buzzed across the sky . . .
The dog woke up and chased the squirrel!

When the dog woke up and chased the squirrel . . .
The robin flew into the tree!

When the robin flew into the tree . . .
The leaf blew in!